Valentine's Day

Story and pictures by Miriam Nerlove

ALBERT WHITMAN & COMPANY
MORTON GROVE, ILLINOIS

For Howard, with much love.

ALSO BY MIRIAM NERLOVE
Christmas
Easter
Halloween
Hanukkah
If All the World Were Paper
Passover
Purim
Thanksgiving

Text and illustrations © 1992 by Miriam Nerlove.
Published in 1992 by Albert Whitman & Company,
6340 Oakton Street, Morton Grove, Illinois 60053-2723.
Published simultaneously in Canada
by General Publishing, Limited, Toronto.
10 9 8 7 6 5 4

Library of Congress Cataloging-in-Publication Data

Nerlove, Miriam.
Valentine's Day: story and pictures/
by Miriam Nerlove
p. cm.
Summary: A brief history of Valentine's
Day is followed by a girl's account of her
celebrations at preschool and at home.
ISBN 0-8075-8454-1 (lib. bdg.)
ISBN 0-8075-8455-X (pbk.)
(1. Valentine's Day–Fiction. 2. Stories
in rhyme.) I. Title.
PZ8.3.N365Val 1992   91-19289
(E)–dc20   CIP
                                                  AC

Hooray! Hooray!
Valentine's Day is on its way.

People say that long ago,
there lived a priest named Valentine.

He was a man with many friends,
for he was brave as well as kind.

Lots of children wrote him notes—
letters that they loved to send.

And then a holiday was named
for Valentine, their special friend.

This holiday, Saint Valentine's,
is coming soon—it's hard to wait.
I mail a card to Grandma's house. . .

and then at school we celebrate!

We make the cards called valentines
with scissors, glitter, crayons, glue.
We cut and color paper hearts.
The teacher helps me write, "For you."

On other cards we write, "Be mine,"
or, "Will you be my valentine?"

The cards go in a fancy box.
Tommy passes them around.

I scoop up all my valentines
and make the most enormous mound!

We hang up streamers and some hearts
and tie balloons up in a bunch.

We eat pink cupcakes—cookies, too.
The teacher pours us cold red punch.

Daddy brings the cake in now—
the one I helped him decorate.

When all the fun at school is done
we bundle up—it's getting late!

At home I give a card to Mom.
I have another one for Dad.

I give one to my brother, too,
and hug him just to make him mad!

Then I give my dog a heart—
a big red card she chews apart.

My family gives me candy hearts
with messages that say, "You're fine,"
"Love you," "Sweetie," "You're cute stuff,"
"Let's be friends," and "Please be mine."

Daddy lifts Mom off the rug.
He gives her flowers and a hug.

Then Daddy holds *me* very tight.
He lifts me high and swings me, too.

"You are my special valentine,"
he says to me, "and I LOVE YOU!"